OUR FRIEND HEDGEHOG

The Story of Us

A Place to Call Home

Our Friend Hedgehog

A PLACE TO CALL HOME

Lauren Castillo

Our Friend Hedgehog

A PLACE TO CALL HOME

Alfred A. Knopf

New York

THIS IS A BORZOI BOOK PUBLISHED BY ALFRED A. KNOPF

Copyright © 2022 by Lauren Castillo
Epigraph art by Afton Kutil

All rights reserved. Published in the United States by Alfred A. Knopf,
an imprint of Random House Children's Books,
a division of Penguin Random House LLC, New York.

Knopf, Borzoi Books, and the colophon are registered trademarks
of Penguin Random House LLC.

Visit us on the Web! rhcbooks.com

Educators and librarians, for a variety of teaching tools,
visit us at RHTeachersLibrarians.com

Library of Congress Cataloging-in-Publication Data
Names: Castillo, Lauren, author, illustrator.
Title: A place to call home / Lauren Castillo.
Description: First edition. | New York: Alfred A. Knopf, 2022. |
Series: Our friend Hedgehog; 2 | Audience: Ages 5–9. |
Summary: "Hedgehog and her friends discover that home can be
found in unexpected places."—Provided by publisher.
Identifiers: LCCN 2021039420 (print) | LCCN 2021039421 (ebook) |
ISBN 978-1-5247-6674-0 (hardcover) | ISBN 978-1-5247-6675-7 (library binding) |
ISBN 978-1-5247-6676-4 (ebook) Subjects: CYAC: Hedgehogs—Fiction. |
Animals—Fiction. | Friendship—Fiction.
Classification: LCC PZ7.C2687244 Pl 2022 (print) |
LCC PZ7.C2687244 (ebook) | DDC [E]—dc23

The illustrations in this book were created using
pen, pencils, watercolor, and Photoshop.

Book design by Martha Rago

MANUFACTURED IN CHINA

10 9 8 7 6 5 4 3 2 1

First Edition

For my friends Afton and Tippett,
who inspired this story

Contents

Families come in all shapes and sizes.
Sometimes they are joined by birth,
and other times they are chosen.
Hedgehog, Mutty, Mole, Owl, Beaver,
Hen and Chicks, and me, Annika Mae.
We may look different on the outside,
but together we are like family.
Together we are home.

Between the great forests, in the center of the river, on a teeny-tiny island, lived two dear friends: Hedgehog and Mutty.

Most nights they slept on the island, but they spent their days in the company of good friends.

On this day, Hedgehog woke early to a chilly breeze ruffling her spines.

The trees all over Hedge Hollow had changed color weeks ago, and some had lost their leaves. Wintertime was coming very soon.

Wintertime meant snow.

And snow brought with it all sorts of fun.

Snowball fights, snow tubing, and most exciting of all: snowhogs!

Hedgehog had been drafting her
practice snowhog for months.
She'd use two sticks for arms,

two dark pebbles for eyes,
another for the nose, and

at least twenty-eight
small twigs for its spines.

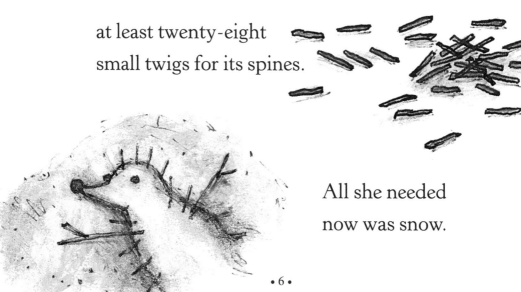

All she needed
now was snow.

Hedgehog tapped on Mutty's shoulder. "Wake up, Mutty! Owl has a new book for us today!"

Owl often hosted story times, and the friends took turns cramming into his tiny loft. Today, it was Hedgehog, Mutty, and Mole's turn.

Hedgehog grabbed Mutty by the paw and
hopped into the little red boat Beaver had
made them. Quickly and carefully, they
rowed toward the mainland.

*I*t was a long walk to Owl's, but by now Hedgehog knew the path well.

Hedgehog zigzagged and sing-sang through the forest, with Mutty in tow.

"Today is new-book day, today is new-book day—Owl is going to read us a new book todaaaay!" she sang out. A songbird whistled back, and then she felt a *plop* on her head.

"Ack! Bird poo!"

Hedgehog shrugged. "Well, at least it's good luck," she giggled.

They continued on the path until they

reached Mushroom Glen. Hedgehog
couldn't believe how many mushrooms
had sprouted since their last visit. She
bent to take a closer look, and a flicker of
movement caught her eye.

Something . . . spiny.

Something . . .
something . . .
much too familiar.

Was it . . . ?

Hedgehog grabbed Mutty and
ran as fast as she could to Owl's.
She didn't look back,
even once.

"Owl! Owl!" Hedgehog yelled. "I saw
a . . . ME!"

"You what?" Owl yelled back down.
"You saw you?"

"No, I saw something that looked just
like me! It had my same
spines and my same
snout, and it was just
about my size!"

"Most
likely it
was your reflection," Owl said.

"But it couldn't have been my
reflection, Owl! I wasn't
near any water."

"Hmm. Maybe just a pinecone?" Owl
suggested.

"But it was walking!" urged
Hedgehog.

Owl glided down from his loft and Mole
followed.

"Ciao, amici," greeted Mole. "Tell us
exactly what happened."

Hedgehog was still shaking from the
incident. "I—I was in Mushroom Glen.
I looked up, and there was a face just
like mine. That's all I can tell you. . . .
I didn't stick around for long!"

"Goodness gracious!" Mole said. "Did
you talk to it?"

"No," said Hedgehog. "I was too startled
to say anything."

"I have a theory," said Owl. "It heard
about my fantastic read-aloud and wanted
to trick us by taking your place today!"

"Hmmmm," said Mole. "But if it wanted

to come to story time, why was it all the way
down at Mushroom Glen?"

"True . . . ," said Owl.

He began flipping through a large book.

"What are you doing?" Hedgehog asked.

"Finding your answer," Owl declared.

He turned the book around so they could all see. "It seems you've met your doppelganger!"

"My doppel-*who?*"

"Doppelganger," Mole repeated. "That's a German word."

Owl nodded, reading aloud from his dictionary: " 'Doppelganger: *a ghostly double or counterpart of a living person.*' "

"What?" Hedgehog felt faint.

"Don't worry so much," Owl said. "All it means is there's a Hedgehog look-alike out there. . . ."

"Or maybe it's just a relative," Mole cut in, seeing Hedgehog's worried face. "A long-lost sister or cousin."

Alone with Mutty on the tiny island, Hedgehog had often wondered what it would be like to have a big family.

"I suppose it might be nice to meet a relative . . . ," Hedgehog mused.

"Then let's go!" hooted Owl.
"Doppelganger or no, we're gonna find this
creature."

On the other side of the river, Annika Mae
was helping Beaver.

"Pass me those two long branches,"
Beaver called from a large hole in the
riverbank.

Annika Mae was trying to give Beaver
space to do what he did best, but it had been
her idea to build the Friend Fort. And
Beaver wouldn't let her do any of the
building!

"Beaver, can't I come in and help?"
Annika Mae asked.

"Nope, nope," Beaver replied. "Beavers

only on the construction site. It's too dangerous for anyone else."

"Fiiiine." Annika Mae sighed. "But at least let me pick out the materials. I have a good eye for design."

"You can *design* the inside once I'm done with all the heavy lifting," Beaver said.

Annika Mae was about to object when
something caught her attention.

It looked like the start of one of Hen's "treasure" heaps.

"Hen, are you nearby?" Annika Mae called.

A minute later, Hen came waddling out of the marsh grass with a wingload of junk.

"Annika Mae, lookit all the decorations I found for the fort!" Hen clucked.

"These are, um, *interesting* decorations,"
said Annika Mae, holding up an enormous
pair of indigo underwear.

Hen grabbed the undies back.

"This is a flag! For the fort!" She waved
the undies high and gave a crisp salute.

Annika Mae laughed so hard she snorted,
and soon she was helping Hen search for the
perfect flagpole.

Down the river, just out of sight, there was a big *splat!* Then another. Followed by a "Peep! Peep! Peeeeeeep!" echoing across the riverbank.

"Oh, Chicks," squawked Hen. "March your fluffy feathered fannies over here right this instant!"

The chicks came bouncing through the marsh, covered beak to claw in mud.

"What a mess!" cried Hen. "Go clean that mud off. Don't make me tell you twice."

The chicks dove right off the trash heap and into the river. The water was cold! And the chicks were shivering when they got out.

"Chicks! It's sweater weather.

"Too cold not to wear clothes this time of year," Annika Mae said.

"I don't have a sweater." Beaver's voice echoed from inside the fort.

"I was talking to the chicks!"

Annika Mae hollered back.

"Oh. Well, I thought you should know I don't have one. And I want one. The kind with the buttons and a collar . . ."

Beaver popped his head out the fort entrance. "And if you're wondering what colors, I'm thinking maybe a nice red and purple."

Annika Mae's brow furrowed as she looked down at her own sweater.

"Are you asking for *my* sweater, Beaver?"

"Well, if you don't want it anymore. Sure, I'll take it. . . ."

"Beaver, Abuela made me this. I can't give it away!"

Beaver's face fell.

"But . . . maybe I can ask her to make another one for you?"

"Nah, that's okay," mumbled Beaver. "I don't like to match."

Beaver disappeared once again inside the fort.

As the shivering chicks huddled under their mother's wings, Annika Mae headed up the hill in a hurry. She had some sweater hunting to do.

"**A** hammer and two nails!" Beaver called from inside the fort.

"Helloooo? Annika Mae. I need the hammer and nails NOW!"

"Annika Maaae?"

"Okay, okay, you can come inside if you really want to. . . ."

Beaver huffed out of the fort right as Hedgehog was walking past.

"Hedgehog! You're just in time. Annika Mae disappeared and I need help! Can you lend a paw?"

Hedgehog looked Beaver straight in the eye.

"Heyyy, those are *my* goggles!" Beaver exclaimed.

Without a word, Hedgehog turned away and shuffled upstream.

"Where are you going?!" Beaver yelled. But Hedgehog was already gone.

Beaver sat on the bank, sulking, until the others returned. The chicks bobbled along in little sweaters that Annika Mae had borrowed from one of her dolls. They cheeped and leaped all over Beaver until his frown turned upside down.

Mole, Owl, and Hedgehog arrived just in time to join the chicks in a Beaver tackle.

Over time, the friends had learned that Beaver's grumpy moods were no match for a big group hug.

"That's enough!" shrieked Beaver, hiding his happiness under a paw. "Everyone's here—time to work on the fort!"

"I'm afraid we have an urgent matter to discuss," Owl cut in.

"What could be more urgent than the fort?" Beaver fussed.

"There's another hedgehog in the hollow, and we need to find it."

"Another hedgehog?!" Annika Mae perked up. "How exciting!"

"I agree," said Mole, "but I'm not sure *our* Hedgehog feels the same."

Hedgehog retold the story of the doppelganger. And how, on one paw, she was curious,

but on the other paw, she was frightened to meet another hedgehog.

"I'm exhausted just thinking about it," sighed Hedgehog, curling up on the bank.

"It's okay, tomodachi." Mole put her paw over Hedgehog's paw. "We will be there with you to meet this hedgehog."

"Will you help too, Beaver?" Hedgehog asked hopefully. "We can cover more ground in your raft."

"Of course he will!" Annika Mae piped in. Beaver turned to look at the partially finished fort. "But I was just about to install the door. Without the door, who will keep out intruders?"

"Beaver!" squawked Owl.

Beaver looked back at Hedgehog. She hadn't helped *him* earlier. Why should he help her?

"This could be Hedgehog's family we're talking about," Owl pressed.

"The fort will be in good hands while you're gone." Annika Mae grinned.

"Okaaay," Beaver sighed. "I will take you to look for this doppel-whatever. But let's be quick so we can come back and finish the fort!"

Owl, Mole, Hedgehog, and Mutty boarded the raft.

"Bon voyage!" Annika Mae waved as they launched into the choppy river waters.

"What are we looking for again?" Beaver asked as he began paddling.

"Do you ever listen?" Owl hooted. "We are looking for Hedgehog's doppelganger. Her look-alike."

"Is that why you were too busy to help with the fort earlier?" Beaver groused. "And why did you need my safety goggles?!"

"What are you talking about, Beaver?" Hedgehog looked puzzled.

"I saw you, Hedgehog. You were headed around that bend." Beaver pointed past his dam.

"Beaver, compadre, Hedgehog has been with us all morning. It couldn't have been her," said Mole.

For a moment, everyone just looked at each other in confusion.

"The doppelganger!" cried Owl. "It must have been the doppelganger."

"Are you *sure* it went that direction?" asked Mole.

"Captain Beaver is *always* sure," Beaver boasted.

Owl rolled his eyes. "Let's go!" he urged.

Beaver worked hard to paddle upstream against the current. Hedgehog and Mole were

huddled together, each gripping one of
Mutty's arms.

As they approached the dam, Beaver called
to the friends, "Time to get out and push!"

"Push wha—" Owl began to ask.

"No time for questions. Out, out!" Beaver ordered as he paddled his raft right up to the bank.

"Ready, set, PUSH!"

The crew pushed as Beaver pulled. Finally, the raft was around the other side of the beaver dam and back in the water.

"Quivering quails, I'm beat!" Mole collapsed to the ground. The friends flopped down next to her.

"It's not *that* heavy," chuckled Beaver. "Now come on, we better keep moving if you want to find this other hedgehog before dark."

They dragged themselves back onto the

raft, and Beaver continued paddling as they entered unfamiliar forest.

"I've never been up here," Hedgehog called over the noisy current.

A movement in the distance caught Owl's eye. "Beaver, steer toward that hedgerow," ordered Owl.

"Hey, who's the captain here?" Beaver snapped, but turned the raft toward the long row of bushes.

Owl took flight, circling the area once,

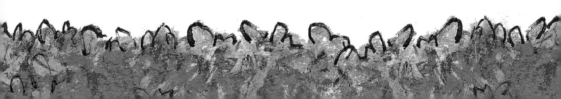

twice, then thrice.

"As I suspected," Owl said when he
returned. "There are hedge*hogs* behind the
hedge*row.* Lots of 'em."

Hedgehog's stomach flipped. She held
Mutty even tighter now.

Mole noticed and put an arm around her
shoulder.

Swiftly and surely, they rowed straight
toward the hedgerow.

Beaver, Owl, Mole, and Hedgehog, who was clinging to Mutty, tiptoed toward the hedgerow.

They peered through the leaves to see what was on the other side.

"Afternoon, mates!" A raspy voice startled them.

Hedgehog whirled around and found herself snout to snout with her own mirror image!

But as Hedgehog studied the creature, she realized they didn't look *exactly* alike.

This hedgehog had white whiskers on its face.

Its nose was a bit pointier.

And it looked wobbly on its feet.

"H-hi," Hedgehog stammered.

"I don't think we've met," the other hedgehog said. "The name's Grandhog."

"Hello, sir." Owl extended a wing. "My

name is Owl. These are my friends Beaver,
Mole, and Hedgehog."

Grandhog looked directly at Hedgehog.
"You checking in?" he asked.

"Checking in?" Hedgehog questioned.

"To Hedge Hideaway," Grandhog said.
"The place where all our kind come to
hibernate."

"Hibernate?" Hedgehog still didn't understand.

"Hibernate," repeated Owl. *"To spend the winter sleeping."*

Grandhog puffed out his chest. "Hedge Hideaway is the best hibernation retreat. I built it with my own two paws."

Beaver looked impressed. "Can we have a tour?" he asked.

"Sure, mate," answered Grandhog. "Follow me."

When Beaver, Owl, Mole, and Hedgehog stepped through the hedgerow, there was a whole village—rows and rows of tiny houses, and *lots* of hedgehog look-alikes scurrying about! They were carrying bags and bundles into their houses.

Owl was reading the names off the doors:
" 'Heatherhog, Howardhog, Harperhog,
Hectorhog, Hugohog, Hildahog.' "
Hedgehog could hardly believe her eyes.
   Grandhog read the large sign at the
entrance:

HOME IS WHERE THE HEDGE · HEART IS

"Whatcha think now?" Grandhog asked Hedgehog. "Great place to hibernate, eh?"

"Umm. Sure," Hedgehog squeaked. She had never hibernated before. A nap that lasted the whole winter sounded *way* too long.

As Beaver asked Grandhog questions about the tiny houses, Hedgehog whispered over to Mole, "Mole, do I *have* to hibernate?"

Mole patted Hedgehog on the back. "You don't have to do anything you don't want to do, dear."

Normally, Mole's steady words helped calm Hedgehog, but this was different. If all hedgehogs were supposed to hibernate, and if Hedge Hideaway was the best place *to* hibernate, that meant Hedgehog should stay, didn't it?

"Look, Hedgehog," said Beaver, "there's only one empty hedge-house left."

"Does it look like home?" Mole asked.

"Well . . ." Hedgehog hesitated.

"It's up to you." Grandhog smiled. "But it's first come, first served here at Hedge Hideaway.

"Tonight we have our annual Hibernation Feast. A large community meal before the big sleep. You can get to know your neighbors there. Not that you'll see them much during hibernation." Grandhog chuckled.

Hedgehog knew that staying the winter at Hedge Hideaway meant not seeing her friends. Not playing with them in the snow. Not going to Owl's read-alouds.

But at Hedge Hideaway she'd be among her own kind.

She repeated Grandhog's words in her
head: *Home is where the hedge-heart is.
Well, I am a hedgehog. So I guess this is
supposed to be home.* Hedgehog's heart
wasn't quite feeling it yet, but maybe this
place would begin to feel like home soon.

"Okay, I will stay," said Hedgehog to
Grandhog.

"Brilliant!" Grandhog gave her a slap on
the back as her friends stood in silence.

"We are going to miss you, Hedgehog,"
Mole said after a somber pause.

"Exceedingly," Owl said with a nod.

"Yup, yup," muttered Beaver.

"But I'll see you once hibernation is over," Hedgehog said, forcing a smile.

"Yes. We will come to pick you up," said Mole in a more cheerful tone.

Hedgehog walked Owl, Beaver, and

Mole back to the raft. She hugged them quickly, holding back her tears as they piled on. Hedgehog squeezed Mutty tight to her chest as she watched her friends drift downstream, far away from Hedge Hideaway. Far away from her.

A CREATIVE SURPRISE

While the others were gone, Annika Mae, Hen, and Chicks were occupied with very important Friend Fort business.

The chicks marched around the fort, keeping guard. "Cheep. Cheep. Cheep-cheep-cheep!"

Inside the fort, Hen and Annika Mae were admiring the shelves Beaver had carved with his teeth. "Beaver is an excellent woodworker!" Hen clucked.

"Yes, and he knows it!" Annika Mae laughed.

Beaver hadn't hung all the shelves yet,

so Annika Mae decided to surprise him. How hard could it be to hang up a shelf?

"Hen, would you hold this bracket while I hammer?"

"That sounds easy," said Hen, taking her place.

As Annika Mae swung the hammer, Hen shrieked, "My wing!" and dropped the bracket.

"I wasn't going to hit your wing!" Annika Mae said. "If you're going to help, you'll need to hold still."

"Okay, okay," agreed Hen, "let's try again."

This time, Hen did not let go. But the sound that came out of her beak frightened Annika Mae so terribly that she struck too hard, splitting the bracket right in half.

"Oh no!" Annika Mae cried. "I broke it!"

Hen picked up the other bracket. "But look, there's another."

"I know, Hen, but we need *two* brackets to hang the shelf. One won't work." Annika Mae pouted.

Hen felt bad. "Oh. Well, finding things *is* my specialty," she said. "I can find you another brackamajiggy."

Hen waddled outside and began sorting through her treasure pile, Annika Mae following behind.

"Nah . . ."

"Won't do . . ."

"Too clunky . . ."

"Too flimsy."

Annika Mae began to lose hope.

Hen disappeared under the pile, and when she came back, she was wearing a wooden fruit crate.

"This!" she cheered. "This is exactly what we need."

"I don't think so, Hen," Annika Mae said

doubtfully. "That is not a bracket."

"I have a vision," said Hen with a twinkle in her eye. "Do you trust me?"

Annika Mae was a little skeptical, but she had never seen Hen so excited.

"Okay, Hen," she said. "Let's give it a try."

Hedgehog sat Mutty down inside their new home. It didn't feel very homey. If she was going to stay here all winter, she'd better cozy things up.

Outside her window, other hedgehogs were lugging leaves and straw into their houses.

"I'll be right back, Mutty."

Hedgehog smiled at a few kind faces along the way, and they smiled back. It felt strange to see so many hedgehogs in one place when only yesterday she hadn't seen even *one* other hedgehog.

As she walked home with an armload
of leaves and nesting grasses, she noticed
the sky. It was layered with cotton-candy
clouds.

She felt the air. Still and cold. Was it going
to snow?! She was so excited that she ran all
the way back to her tiny house.

"Mutty! Snow!" Hedgehog grabbed
Mutty and brought him outside to see the
sky. "Well, it's not snowing yet," she told
him. "But I don't want to miss the first
flakes!"

Then she heard Grandhog's
voice echoing over a
loudspeaker:

"*Attention, hibernators!*

Due to an incoming snowstorm, we have decided to begin the annual Hibernation Feast a little early. Please join us in the picnic area before sunset. Toodles!"

"I was right!" Hedgehog cheered. "The first snow really is on its way!"

She gave Mutty a squeeze.

"Let's go make some new friends."

Hedgehog was in such a hurry to get to the feast, she stumbled over a stick in the path. *Oooh, this would make a perfect snowhog arm!* she thought.

When Hedgehog and Mutty arrived at the feast, it was even grander than Hedgehog had imagined. New faces always made her nervous, and there must have been a hundred in this room alone! She looked for empty seats but didn't see even one.

Then Hedgehog heard a familiar raspy voice. She turned to see Grandhog beaming her way.

"Greetings, Hedgehog! Quite an impressive spread, eh? Here, let me find you a seat."

Grandhog walked Hedgehog and Mutty over to the very last empty seat. He looked at Mutty and then back to Hedgehog.

"I'm sorry, only one seat left," Grandhog apologized.

"Thanks, Grandhog." Hedgehog smiled anxiously and took a seat at the table, placing Mutty and the snowhog stick on her lap.

"Enjoy the roast turnip, it's my favorite!"

Grandhog called as he scuttled away,
leaving Hedgehog among strangers.

  Hedgehog looked around. There was so
much food, the wood planks bowed under
the weight of it all. There were plump
strawberries and long sprigs of cranberries,
whole carrots and yellow squash, dandelion

greens and roasted asparagus, blueberry
tarts and purple sweet potato pie. Hedgehog
had never eaten a rainbow before!

"Hi, my name is Heatherhog," said one

of Hedgehog's tablemates, noticing her surprise. "You must be a first-timer at Hedge Hideaway."

"You are right," Hedgehog giggled nervously. "My name is Hedgehog, and this is Mutty."

"Nice to meet you." Heatherhog extended her paw. "This hog stuffing his face is Hugohog."

"Howdy!" Hugohog mumbled through a mouthful of strawberries.

"Howdy," Hedgehog repeated back. There was a pause. Hedgehog didn't know what to say. Then she remembered the stick on her lap.

"I was wondering . . . ," Hedgehog ventured.

"Do you like to build snowhogs?"

"Snowhogs?" Hugohog questioned.

"I mean, when it snows—do you like to build hedgehogs out of snow?"

"Ohh. Snowhogs!" Hugohog guffawed. "No way, y'all. I never go in the snow. It's too cold for a thin-blooded fella like me."

"My favorite thing about snow is *sleeping* through it," snorted Heatherhog.

The two were laughing, but Hedgehog didn't get the joke. How could they not like snow?

For the rest of the meal, Hedgehog munched carrots and cranberries while listening to the others chitchat about hibernation. Not even *one* liked snow. Every hedgehog sounded so happy to sleep

through the entire winter. They would miss
snowball fights, snow tubing, and most
important of all, snowhogs. Hedgehog
could not imagine sleeping through all of
that! These hedgehogs might be made of
the same spines and snouts, but their hearts
spoke different languages.

Back inside her tiny house, Hedgehog built a nest out of leaves and straw, and curled up against Mutty.

She thought about the snow that would soon arrive.

She pictured the happy faces of the other hedgehogs at Hedge Hideaway.

She wished for that kind of happiness again—the kind she shared with her friends.

A CHANGE OF PLANS

It was just after dawn when a cold draft
jolted Hedgehog awake. She bounced out of
bed and straight to the window. The world
outside was as white as a new sheet of paper.
It was *snow*! Actual snow. Softly falling
from the sky and blanketing the ground.
It was the most
beautiful sight
she had ever seen.

Hedgehog
leaped out the
door.

She scooped up

pawfuls of snow and launched
them in the air as high as she
could.

Then she packed a huge snowball,
scrambled to the top of a snowdrift,
and tossed it into the sky.

Plunk! Her snowball
bounced off the welcome
sign, knocking some
snow off and revealing
the words Grandhog

had spoken yesterday: HOME IS WHERE THE
HEDGE-HEART IS.

Hedgehog listened to her heart. This time
it was louder than before.

She slid down the snow hill and raced
inside.

Leaf by leaf, Hedgehog built a map. It went all the way from Hedge Hideaway to the Friend Fort. When Grandhog and the others came out of hibernation, they would know exactly where to visit her.

She turned to Mutty. "Let's go home."

The white snow brightened their path as Hedgehog carried Mutty downriver. Hers were the only footprints as far as the eye could see.

Once they reached Beaver's dam, they stopped to take a short break. Snow was still falling all around them.

"If this keeps up, we'll have to tunnel our way home!" Hedgehog told Mutty.

They continued on their way.

Hours passed, and the snow made it difficult to see ahead. Finally Hedgehog heard the faint sound of voices. Then up in the sky she spotted Owl circling among the falling flakes.

"Mutty, we are almost home!" she called.

With each step, the voices of her dear friends got louder and clearer.

"Gotcha!" she heard Beaver chuckle.

They were having a snowball fight!

Hedgehog ducked into the brush and snuck as quietly as she could sneak. She scooped up a pawful of snow and packed it tight. Then she hurled it at Beaver, hitting him square between the eyes.

"Oof! Beaver down!" Beaver fell backward into the snow.

The rest of the friends spun around in surprise.

"Umngani! You came back!" Mole cheered.

"Peep! Peep!" the chicks cheeped.

Beaver popped up. "I knew you'd come back." He grinned. "Also, nice throw," he

whispered, leaning in. "You can be on my
team."

Owl swooped down, flapping his wings
with excitement. "Hedgehog! You're just in
time for the first story time in our new fort."

"We're waiting on Annika Mae to finish
her *design*," Beaver grumbled. "She won't
let us inside until she and Hen are ready for
their 'big reveal.'"

Hedgehog was exhausted from her journey. She wanted nothing more than to curl up, but there was something she had to do first.

"While we wait for story time, I have something I want to show you!" Hedgehog exclaimed.

"Ooooh, a surprise?" Owl called.

"Yes! But I could use some help."

Hedgehog sent the friends for supplies.

While they were off collecting, Hedgehog carefully built her very first snowhog.

She knew exactly how to make it, thanks to all the drafting she had done on her island.

Owl brought two sticks.

Beaver fetched a pile of twigs.

And Mole and Chicks each returned with
one pebble.

Hedgehog placed lots of spines,

two arms,

two eyes,

and one nose.

She stepped back to admire her creation.

"Well, look at that!" Owl hooted. "I see what it is now."

"It's YOU!" Beaver whooped.

"It's a snowhog." Hedgehog blushed.

"It's absolutely marvelous!" praised Mole.

The friends gave Hedgehog a big round of applause. A split second later, the Friend Fort door flew open.

"What's all this commotion?" Hen clucked. Then she spotted Hedgehog, and her eyes grew wide with delight.

"You are home!" Hen announced. "Annika Mae! Hedgehog is home!"

Annika Mae dove through the Friend Fort door, squeezing Hedgehog and Mutty so hard, their insides nearly became their outsides.

"I missed you both so much," she cooed.

Hedgehog felt her heart swell. There was no place else she'd rather be.

"Well, now that everyone is here, shall
we reveal the Friend Fort?" Annika Mae
smiled.

"We've only been waiting all day!"
Beaver harrumphed.

"Okay, Mr. Impatient, you can
help me with the ribbon cutting."
Annika Mae pulled a long red
ribbon out of her pocket.

"To celebrate the official opening of our amazing new clubhouse: a place we can all call home."

Beaver took one end of the ribbon and stretched it across the fort entrance.

"Hedgehog, would you do the honors?" Annika Mae handed her a pair of scissors.

Hedgehog cut the ribbon right in the center, and everyone cheered triumphantly.

"Okay, NOW can we see the fort?" Beaver persisted.

"Yes, Beaver. But close your eyes before you go in."

One by one the friends filed into the fort.

"Okay, on the count of three, open them. One . . . two . . . three!"

"Oooh!" they all gasped. "Aaaaah!"

Owl fluttered to the bookcase. "Look at all these *books*!"

"And you did it without my help." Beaver nodded with approval.

There was a hodgepodge of pillows and poufs and even a perch for Owl. Most importantly, there were enough seats for everyone. They sat down and looked around, taking it all in.

"There's one last surprise," Annika Mae announced, reaching for a bag. "Since it's winter now, you each need something warm to wear."

She pulled out a ball of scarves.

"Blue for Mole, orange for Owl, teal for Hen. A peach one for Hedgehog—"

"Well, what'd you get me?" Beaver interrupted.

"Beaver! That's rude," squawked Owl.

Annika Mae grinned. "Do you want to see what I got you, Beaver?"

"I thought you'd never ask," Beaver said with a half smile.

Annika pulled the purple-and-red-striped sweater she had worn yesterday out of the bag. "For you," she said with a smile. "I have plenty of clothes, and I know Abuela would be happy for you to have it."

Beaver's face flushed with happiness as he put on his new sweater.

"Attention, everyone!" Owl called. "The time has come for the first-ever Friend Fort read-aloud!"

Annika Mae, Hedgehog, Mutty, Mole, Beaver, and Hen and Chicks gathered around. Everyone was cozied up in their new clothes, inside the fort they had created together. They might look different on the outside, but in their hearts, they were family.

Hedge Hollow

Beaver's Dam

Hen and Chic

Owl's
Lookout

Hedgehog's
Island